MEET RUBEN KANE

For: Jack Byrd

Acknowledgment

Inspiration comes in many forms, dreams, walks in the

Park, or just sitting around having a beer. I found

Mine at the basketball court.

Thanks Ruben

Other Books by this Author

Enlisted at 14… A Memoir

Enlisted at 14…And the Journey Continues

Willow…A Novel

Just a Dream

Willow…and the Medusa

Enlisted at 14…Looking Back

Copyright © **2019 by Eddie J Martin**

All rights reserved.

Published in **the USA**

ISBN-9780990544050

The beginning:

Tuesday morning 8:45 AM, Ruben was having breakfast with his wife, of late they hadn't been getting along so well, for some years really. Why they stay together was anybody's guess. They didn't sleep in the same bedroom, if they did have sex it was like the old prizefighter's, meet in a neutral corner.

This morning along with the coffee, Smalltalk over the local newspaper. Who's lying about what, local corruptions, water bill not being passed? Farmers up in arms, in 1938 the threat of war with Germany, there're raisin hell in Belgium already. The economy going downhill so what else is new.

I need to get out of here so I can get down to the office, it's been a month now without a client. I'm a finder, sleuth, Detective, whatever as long as I get paid. Haven't seen my girlfriend in three days now so I know she's pissed. Freda and I have been seeing each other two years now, she knows my situation and I know hers. I met Freda in the park while running, I needed to lose a few pounds. I'm 6 foot one and 235 pounds at 42 years old I thought that was a little much so I was told that running would help. One day along came Freda and we hooked up. She was no spring chicken but at 45 years of age, about 5 foot six and 145 pounds she wasn't bad, I've seen worse. One thing for sure we both needed the work out. The thing about Freda and I is that I could talk to her and that It's never any shit. Except maybe when I didn't see her enough and that's every day if it was up to her, but I like the old girl.

I worked about 12 miles from home in downtown Cleveland Ohio, I live on the west side of town. My office is in a twenty-story building on the 13th floor, two rooms, lounge

and my office. When you walk in there's the lounge with my secretary and her desk to the left and to the right is a couch and table and chair. Some old books I picked up, Life magazines mostly. Out of the lounge is the door connected to my office. My desk is facing the door with a large window behind me looking 13 stories down on Lincoln Boulevard and the trolley cars that are contently passing.

Two halfway decent chairs in front of the desk plus file cabinet, a few pictures around the wall of jazz artist, Billy Holiday, Charlie Parker and Lena Horn. No couch, been meaning to get one just never got around to it. Some nights I'll stay over so I just use the one in the lounge. My desk has the usual stuff in it but then there is the essentials. Smith & Wesson 38 caliber pistol, fifth of Jim Bean, little black book, the rest is just bullshit. Papers on my last case, phone numbers I haven't put in the Rolodex yet, plan paper and two stubby pencils. That reminds me, I have to get down to Woolworth's five & dime department store and pick up a few things for the office. I would ask my Sec., but since I haven't paid her in almost a month, I don't think I should ask her right now. A few weeks ago, I was able to buy a three-year-old Buick that set me back some, but I was really tired of riding those damn trolleys, especially in the winter. Ruben walked into his office and saw his secretary (Rita) Haden made it in yet, Rita was of Mexican descent who had come in the states illegal three years earlier. 5 foot five and just as wide and talk plenty shit. She's been coming in later and later. I guess it'll be that way until she gets paid. That means I'll have to make my own coffee, I'm a heavy coffee drinker at least 10 cups a day. During the evening I may add a little Jim Bean to keep me alive. As I was about to make some coffee the phone rang.

Ruben Kane private eye, can I help you? My husband has been missing for a week now, I've put in a police report three days after he went missing no results as of yet. A friend suggested I contact you.

Whom am I speaking to Ruben said and who is your husband?

Oh, I'm sorry. I'm Mrs. Johanna Studier Bold of the Nuts and Bolts Studiers. Norman Studier owns the company and he's my father. Nathan Bold is my husband.

At hearing that Ruben had to sit down. Naturally he had heard of the Studiers, they own half of Cleveland and had a down payment on the other half. All he could see was dollar signs. So how can I help you Mrs. Studier? Or would you rather be called by your married name.

Mrs. Studier will do just fine, she said. And

You can find my husband Mr. Kane, money is no object.

Ruben smiled and raised his left fist (yes). Well Mrs. Studier my rates are $50 per day plus expenses. Of course, his original rates were only 25 per day but what the hell she can pay it. I'll need three days in advance. That's fine Mr. Kane, I'll send my chauffeur over with the money and all the particulars on Nathan. And when can I expect the (he started to say money) driver? This afternoon Mr. Kane say about 2:30.

 May I asked who referred you to me Mrs. Studier? Yes, you may, a Mr. Webb worth president of the bank of Cleveland. I'll be in touch Mr. Kane.

Webb worth, that's been over a year ago. His wife had gotten picked up by some thugs who held her hostage trying to get him to open his bank's safe. They wanted no police involvement, so he calls me in, which was a referral also. Things worked out well for Webb worth and his family, not so well for the thugs. Three in, three out. Well I'll be damned, Webb worth! He is the only reason I can afford this office space for as long as

I wanted, he said. No rent! The outer door open and Rita walked in, I know, I know I'm late. Take it out of my pay that I haven't received in a month. Now don't give me no shit. Is the coffee made yet?

It's been waiting on you Rita, and I have good news.

I hope so, I'm down to my last pair of nylons.

We got a job, should be getting paid this afternoon.

Hallelujah, Rita said.

At 2:25 PM Rita called him on his intercom and told him that the chauffeur for Mrs. Studier was in the office. Ruben told her to send him right in. The chauffeur was a small black guy no more than 5 foot three, black hat, uniform and white shirt with black bow tie. Mr. Kane I'm Rodney the chauffeur, Mrs. Studier sent me, you've been expecting me? He said.

Yes, I have Rodney, Ruben said, you have something for me? Rodney handed Rubin a large sealed envelope, Ruben thanked him and he left.

Ruben wasted no time in opening the envelope, inside was $500 in cash plus papers on the husband, Nathan. Date of birth, mother's maiden name, father's name, known friends, hangout spots, old girlfriends, etc. Race: black/Puerto Rican. No wonder she came to me Ruben thought. One black dude can always find another. Ruben call Rita into his office and told 14 gave her a month's pay plus a little something extra and told her to take the rest of the day off (She only receives twenty- five dollars a week). He calls Freda and told her that they were going to dinner that night. Meanwhile he thought that he would use the rest of his time going over the papers of the husband and making phone calls.

On the way to meet Freda that evening he stopped at the service station told the attendant to fill it up and check under the hood and also check the tires, while he went into the restroom. When he returned, he notices that his windshield wasn't clean he told the attendant, hey, what's the deal with the windshield? You guys getting a little lax on your job around here, I may find me another station. After the attendant finished all his tasks, he told Ruben what the bill would be, $4.75.

Hey, Ruben said. How much is this gas? $.30 a gallon the attendant said.

You guys trying to get rich Ruben said. I know damn well I'm changing stations now. Hell, the attendant said. You think that's high, in a few more years it'll be at $.57 a gallon.

Oh, hell no, Ruben said. I'll start walking again if that happens.

Freda was waiting at the diner when he got there, she was usually the first to arrive at any function they went to. Geneva's was a barbecue Rib and steak joint with a small bar that played live jazz music on Wednesdays, Fridays and Saturdays. This was a Tuesday so no music this night, but the jukebox did just fine, I put a couple Nickels in the box before I walked over to join Freda and up jumped Billy holiday singing {strange fruit}, the other coin I played was Earl Bostic the great saxophone player. My kind of sounds. Freda was at our favorite table over near the bandstand, don't know how she did that there was a nice dinner crowd for a Tuesday, maybe that's why she gets to the place early.

Hey babe, he said. You're looking nice, and she was.

Thank you, Ruben, now what's the occasion? You get a job or something Freda said.

I did, and I start today but first I had to take my favorite girl out to dinner.

What kind of job is it Freda ask?

Oh, just a little lost and found, I should have it wrapped up within a few days.

I sure hope it's not like that last job you were on with that banker, you really had me scared on that one Freda said.

This one will be nothing like that, just finding a woman's husband that's gone missing. Piece of cake! You ready to order? Ruben said.

You didn't have to get up, Ruben said. I thought we could stay in bed a little longer. I know how you love your coffee and you should have had enough after last night Freda said.

I never get enough of you babe, you know that. Stop your bull shit and get up, breakfast is almost ready plus I have to get to work. Freda was a clerk at a dry cleaners and part owner, settlement from her ex-husband. One grown son who's in the military and station in Hawaii.

After breakfast Ruben made plans to see Freda when he could and headed for his office. This time Rita was there, good morning Mr. Kane there is a few messages for you. I put them on your desk.

Mr. Kane! It's a wonder what a paycheck does to a person's Personality.

Thank you, Rita, Ruben said.

He walked into his office set down at his desk and shortly Rita came in with a cup of coffee.

Damn! I'm gonnia have to pay this woman on time more often.

First message was from my policy man: Ruben that 756 hit for you last night, you got $75 coming to you. Let me know if you're playing tonight and I'll take it out the 75.

Second message was from Dallas, a girl he met on his last case: did you forget my number? Call me!

Third message was from Raymond. You've been calling around asking about this dude name Nathan, married to that Studier woman? I may have some info for you but it'll cost you. Call me!

Raymond was the local barber on the east side of Cleveland, 79th and Cedar to be exact. He has a small barbershop there, he been there 25 years or more. His clients came from the R and B crowd to the jazz groups to the brothers on the block. Raymond knows everything and everybody. More than once he's pointed me in the right direction.

Raymond was outside his shop having a smoke when I drove up. A large man of about 300 pounds and 6 feet two, back in the day he was a hell of a man but now all what he was has turn to fat although he still demands respect and everyone likes him but then don't everyone like there barber, he's about like a bartender, everyone lay their troubles on them. That's how they happen to know everything and that's why I'm here.

Raymond, what's up, Ruben said. You still hanging in there I see.

Ruben, I haven't seen you in a while, you find yourself another barber?

No, nothing like that Raymond I just never get over this way as much anymore and you know I didn't have any wheels. Well I see you got some now and I must say Ruben you still styling. Fedora on your head, tweed sport coat, gray pants, slip over sweater and those damn Stetson shoes. You always did wear them Raymond said.

I've got my standards Raymond if I don't have nothing else Ruben said. You said you had some information for me about this Nathan dude? Ruben said.

You got $10? Raymond said.

Ruben gave Raymond $10 and hope the information was worth it. Your boy was around here about a week ago late wanting a haircut, no one was in the shop and I asked him why he came around so late? Said he had to leave town but couldn't before the bank open the next morning. Didn't you just get married I asked him, where the hell you going? And I asked him, you taking your wife?

Hell, no he said, I got what I want.

Hell, man you got a woman with all that money, what else you need?

How do you make love to a woman and not touch her? He said.

After he said that I was finished cutting his hair and that was the last time I saw him. He did say something about going to the Ebony club when he left.

Raymond that was some good information it should start me on my way to locating him. Well worth the ten clams.

So, where you off to now Raymond asks? To the Ebony club where else Ruben said. Kind of early to be going there isn't it? Raymond said.

There's someone there at all hours and 2 PM I'm sure Tonelli will be there, counting his money.

Tonelli was more than a club owner he was the local pimp with some 20 girls working for him. Slim, 6'2, 185 pounds. Look good in most anything he wore, marcel hairdo with bedroom eyes (so the women say) full mustache. He had five other men working for him and they all dressed similar. Tall felt red hats with trusses. The kind that they wear in Casa Blanca or Cairo, all wore dark suits white shirts and red ties. Old man comforts shoes, you could tell them a mile away. Tonelli and I grew up together but he went one way and I went the other. Far enough away from him that I don't consider us on the same page. Don't get me wrong I do a little dirt here and there but nothing on his level. That is unless I have to.

When T and I were kids stealing hub caps and drinking that Muscatel wine we thought we were it. Skipping school to go to the ballpark. Party's we went to,

Blue light over in the corner of the basement, the five keys singing Earth Angel, couples dancing, more like grinding. Guys hands on girls behind. The dancing then was up close and personal. Very few of us got any drawls at that time but it was a lot of fun going through the motions.

T name back then was Rudolph Rankin Butler, of course no one calls him that anymore. That's when Bullet was kicking ass and taking names. It was T who stopped that. T got a number of us guys together and convinced us that the only way to stop bullet was to get together and beat his black ass, and that's what we did after school one day. Bullet Didn't show up to school for a week after that, a change kid, somewhat, but T's friend forever. For some reason he never liked me and from time to time we still get it on.

His place in the heights is about 10 miles from Raymond's on a main boulevard off 105th and candor. Parking lot for about 150 cars. Canopy to drive under by the front door to discharge passengers. Double doors in front and believe it or not on a couple of nights a week a doorman. Yeah, Tonelli has it going on, riding high, for now!

When you walk in the club you're looking right down a flight of stairs and about 500 yards straight ahead you see the bandstand. Dance floor in front of that and tables all around, White tablecloths and all.

Something he imported from Europe was the telephones on each table so you could call the person at the adjoining table, all were numbered. That was a big hit. The bar took up just about all of the left side of the wall. When I walked in the place it was just about deserted. Bartender behind the bar doing what they do when they're no customers of course they didn't open till eight or nine. 2 to 3 cleanup people, piano player hitting notes of Misty and then there was Bullet sitting at the table near the entrance where Tonelli's office is.

Bullet was about my size he wore the same suit as the rest but could never seem to find one that fit him or he was just one of those guys where whatever he wore didn't look right on him, plus he was ugly. Don't know why Tonelli kept Him around because he wasn't all that smart but he does do whatever "T" tells him to and he did come up with the rest of us. But I can truly say that he was a bully and one mean ass. Still is!

And he don't like me! When coming up we had 3 to 4 fights, I won a couple and lost a couple. Hadn't seen him in years now but I got the feeling he hasn't changed any. When he saw me, his ears perked up like an old bloodhound. He never moved but I saw it in his eyes and of course his ears. I walked up to him and said, bullet! How's it hanging?

You out your neighborhood ain't you Ruben, nothing over here for you.

I missed you too bullet. I need to see T. What makes you think he wants to see you bullet said.

I think you should asked him, he won't like it if he finds out I was here and you never told him, he may even slap your wrist. Ruben, we got to have us another round one day, one day soon. Bullet said.

Yeah, yeah, go fetch your boss.

T baby how's it going? It's been a long time.

Ruben where you been man, you forget your old buds? Bullet didn't give you no hard time did he? T said.

No more than usual Ruben said.

What brings you to this part of town, you hard up? Need a loan or something?

No T, I'm on a job trying to locate someone and thought you could help me out.

You still doing that old detective bull shit? Do you make any money at that?

Not enough T, but the guy I'm searching for is name...

Nathan Boyd, T said. Married to that Studier woman. I heard you were looking for him, you know how word gets around. Well, I'm looking for him to. He made off with one of my girls. I sent bullet after his ass but he couldn't find him. I still got the word out on him; the girl was a heavy earner and I want her back. I can't afford to lose her.

Don't bull shit me T, you could let her go and two more just like her and still be doing good.

I could but I won't, what would my rep. be like then?

Did Nathan come to see you before he vanished? He did! He tried to sell me a heap of jewelry but I didn't bite, I had a feeling he hit his old lady up for them. Now I think he took her shit and also my girl and hit the road. Why the hell would she want his ass back anyway T asked?

I don't know, all I do know is she wants him found and willing to pay for him, maybe for the jewelry. Is that all you can tell me Ruben said?

That's it, better hope you find him before me because I'm gonnia fuck him up if I see him first, T said.

What I can't understand is why a man would leave a woman like Mrs. Studier with all that money for a prostitute.

Beats the hell out of me Ruben said.

One more thing T, your girl that Nathan left with, what's her name?

Sylvia, T said. Pretty little thing.

You think I could talk to her roommate?

If you promise me, you're not going to run off with her. T said. (And laugh)

These girls are night people so I know that four in the afternoon would be way too early for them, so I decided to stop for something to eat since I missed lunch. I learn in this kind of business you eat when you can. There was on old railroad car made into a diner that I remember so I stopped there. Pretty good food and at a cheap price. I'm all about the cost, have to be in today's world. Special of the day, was liver and onions, green beans and mash potatoes. Coffee and apple pie. All for $2.57, not bad, but still a little pricey.

After dinner and Tipping the waitress $.25 I departed the diner for my car. On the way someone call my name.

Ruben, Ruben Kane! I thought that was you, I haven't seen you in a while. The person that was talking was another old boy I went to school with, but he dropped out, said school didn't hold nothing for him. Today he looked like a bum really. Old beat up baseball cap on his head, hair sticking out all sides, needing a shave. Beat up sport jacket, wool shirt that has seen better days. And paints that were barely holding on to his waist by a belt that was down to its last notch. , combat boots and he was shaking.

Dodie, how's it been Ruben said?

Not too good Ruben, I kind of hit on bad times but I'm working on a deal that's sure to get me back on track, I just need a small stake. Can you help me?

How much of a stake are we talking about Dodie?

I think $25 should do it Ruben, yeah $25. How about two dollars Dodie, Will two dollars do?

Yeah Ruben, two dollars will do fine.

I gave Dodie the two dollars and thought to myself, $200 wouldn't help the shit Dodie has.

The girl's apartment (house really) was a two Plax with two women living on each side, Chloe lives on the left with use to be roommate Sylvia. I guess she'll be getting a new roomie soon. I walked up the five steps to the porch and knocked on the door and after about two minutes a brunette open up.

You Ruben she asked?

Yes, I said. Did T call you?

Yes, he told me to talk to you, come on in. Chloe was a white dame about five two and hundred and 35 pounds. A turban around her head and wearing a baby Jane nightgown, still, and Slippers. Cute face and nice legs but then she would have to be, the business she's in.

She curled up on the couch with one leg under the other and told me to sit on the other in. I must say that was a nice sight but I had to remember that I was there on business.

Chloe how long had you and Sylvia been roommates? Ruben asks.

Close to six months, you know in this business you don't stay together to long. I was here first then Sylvia, T pulled us both in and we been here ever since. Everything was going great until she met Nathan and fell in love. How did it start between him and Sylvia? Ruben asked.

The usual way, he claimed he wasn't getting any at home so he used Sylvia's services. He'd started using her more and more, one thing led to another and here we are.

You have any idea where they may have gone? Ruben said.

No, and if I had I would have told T and he would have found her by now, Chloe said. You would have told T where she was?

You damn right, you know what's going to happen to her when he finds her? We not close like that. When she told me that she and Nathan was leaving I told her what would happen if T found out but did, she listen, no! Would you mind if I looked through her room?

No, I don't mind, it's the one on the left, Chloe said. As Ruben was looking through Sylvia's room, he saw that it was about cleaned out. Cloths, jewelry, cosmetics, wigs and hairpieces. Ruben looked under the bed, post of the bed, clothes closet floors for loose boards. Chest of drawers and under and behind.

Behind pictures on the wall and chandeliers. Chair cushions and under chairs. After 20 minutes of searching Ruben set down on the bed and shook his head, nothing! He got up and was about to leave when he thought. Hey, I never looked under the mattress. But that's too obvious I know T and the boys looked there. But then T had sent bullet and he's stupid. Ruben looked under the head of the mattress and the frame, nothing. Then he went to the foot, again nothing. On the right side of the bed there it was, under the frame on the cross board, a small red book, a diary? About 4 x 4. I glanced through it and stuck it in my pocket.

As I left Sylvia's bedroom Chloe asked me if I found anything.

No, not a thing I said.

I didn't think so, T's people went over that room and they didn't find a thing either. Who was it that search the room Ruben asked?

Bullet! Chloe said.

I was about to leave the house when Chloe says to me, you know I don't have to be at work for another three hours!

Two hours and 30 minutes later as I was walking out the door Chloe says to me, T said to tell you that this one was on the house.

Ruben turned around and said, thank T for me and thank you too!

Since I couldn't think of anything else to do right then I decided to head back to the office and read through Sylvia's diary. Rita had left but did leave me a note from my policy man and my winnings from the other night. Ms. Studier had call to see if there was any development on Nathan. I see right now she may be a problem. It's only been two days, but then again it is her dime.

I poured myself a cup of coffee and Jim Bean minus the coffee, set at my desk with my feet up and began to read.

It seems that Sylvia started the diary right after she arrived in Cleveland from Montana, country girl. Getting off the bus and not having much money and any place to go she meet this nice-looking black guy that said he could help her; his name was Tonelli. He took me to eat, found a place for me to stay and he said to show her appreciation she should sleep with him. And that's how it started she writes. Eight months and many clients later she met Nathan. After a few engagements he began telling her about his home life I could tell that he was getting very attach to me. I've learned that other than priest, bartenders and Barber's, prostitutes are the next in line to hear confessions. Nathan had met this high society lady whose father had plenty money so they got married but there was a catch. Nathan was black and the father didn't approve of the marriage, to top that his wife was timid, didn't like to be touched. She claims as long as she was taking care of him, he shouldn't have any complaints. He started seeing me once every two weeks then once every week. Then twice a week. One night while in bed he told me about the Jewelry that she had in a safety deposit box and how much was supposed to be in it. His proposal was; he could get into the box and they could head for places unknown.

I wanted to get out the life but didn't know how until now. I think I'll just play him alone until he gets the jewelry then leave him. The diary went on to say, we're meeting at the cabin tonight to discuss when and where.

That shed a lot of light on what went down but I'm wondering where this cabin is she's talking about. Don't sound like any place in town, maybe I'll ask Ms. Studier if her family even have a cabin.

So, it sounds like Sylvia didn't give a damn about Nathan she was just using him to get out the life and make her a few bucks on the side. Makes sense!

I reached in the bottom drawer of my desk and brought out the bottle of Jim Bean, Poured two fingers and put the bottle back.

I need to call Ms. Studier but I think it's a little too late now, maybe in the morning. Too late to call her but not too late to head for a popular club that be open on Wednesday evenings with live jazz music. Coleman Hawkins, the jazz saxophonist was in town and I've been wanting to see and hear him. Midnight is a good time to catch him, I've got a number of 78 RPM records by him and don't want to miss this show. Did all I can do today on Mrs. Studier's case. The Cave was a hole in the wall but the jazz artists seem to like those kind of places. Belowground, smoke filled rooms, close quarter tables, large bar and jam packed. Standing room only even if there were a cover charge of $2.50. I'll pay it to see Coleman and even stand up while I'm doing it. When I got there, he was in the middle of the second set and playing April in Paris.

Bass, piano, and drums completed the quartet. I fought my way over to the bar because I knew it was useless trying to find a waitress and order myself a JB on the rocks. I acknowledge a few people I knew and then concentrated on Coleman. He did a couple more numbers and said they were going on break, back in 15 minutes. I had to relieve myself so I went in the back to the restroom. If you go Straight there is an exit door that leads to the back alley, to the left is the women's rest room and to the right of that is the men's. I walked in and to the urinal and did my business, walked over to the sink and proceeded to wash my hands. The door open and of all the people I didn't want to see at any time was, Bullet!

Well I'll be damned he said, I must be living right, Ruben Kane, of all people. Never figured I'd see you again so soon.

I could tell bullet had more than his share of the sauce this night and I was wondering whether or not I would get out of their without getting my head bashed in. What's up bullet I said? How you enjoying the show?

Fuck you Ruben, I said I was going to kick your ass the next time I saw you, may as well be tonight.

Look bullet I said. Save yourself some grief and forget about it.

Fuck that bullet said and came toward me and threw a right punch at my head, as he was coming at me and throwing his punch there was a dab of water spilled on the floor and he slipped and fell on his ass. So, me being a nice guy and all I kicked him in his head, least

I could do. I headed for the door and he grab my foot and tripped me. I went down and we were both on the floor, he got up first and he kicked me in the ribs. I managed to get up and now we were both on our feet facing each other both in our boxing stance, just like old times. I threw a left to his midsection he counted and caught me on my fore head right above my left eye and my head bounce back, I felt that one. I then throw a right trying to get him off balance but he came back with another right to the same side of my head he hit the first time only this time I went down in the same spot of water he had. On the floor I thought, Bullet has learned some new shit since the last time we got into it, I got to do something about this. So, while I was down, I kicked out and caught him in the balls, he screamed and grab his self and drop to his knees. By that time, I was up and throw a vicious left to the right side of bullets head, he went down, and I felt now would be a good time to vacate. As I was leaving Bullet was getting up still holding his self-cursing and saying, Ruben I'm gonnia kill your ass, and started following me. Instead of going back in the club I headed to the exit door and into the alley. Outside the door I spotted a metal garbage can, picked it up and move to the side of the door and raised it up shoulder high, waiting for him to come out. Hoped he came out first and no one else, if so, oh well! Bullet rushed out the door and Ruben sung the can at his head and connected, bullet momentum took him out into the alley and that's where he laid and that's where he stayed.

Well that's my evening with Coleman Hawkins, at least I still have his records.

Hey boss you been here all-night Rita asked.

I set up on the couch, yawn and said, you make the coffee yet?

No, I just walked in but I'll get right on it. Hey, what happened to your eye? You run into a door or something.

Or something Ruben said. What time is it Ruben asked?

8:30 Rita said. Coffee will be ready in five.

Ruben stood up and almost fell back down, he was hurting all over. That damn bullet has gotten stronger over the years or I've gotten weaker.

There was a small washroom off his office and he went in to clean up, the left side of his head had a nice size lump and his left eye was trying to close on him. He kept a change of clothes, he sure couldn't wear what he had on last night. He'd have to have Rita take them to the cleaners and not the one where Freda works.

Four cups of coffee, four aspirins, three doughnuts and I felt like a new man. Received a call from T and he said and I quote:

Ruben, did you have to fuck up Bullet like you did? Couldn't you just have broken his leg or something like that? I'm told he's going to be laid up for at least a week, now what the hell am I going to do about a bodyguard? Damn you Ruben.

Well I guess I could come over and hang out with you for a week or so but I'm on a job, Ruben said. You do have other people.

Not like bullet, you know that. T said.

I don't know what to say T except keep your head down.

I called Mrs. Studier at one and told her what I found out and asked her about the cabin and she told me that the family did have a cabin about 125 miles outside of Cleveland in harbor County. And Nathan has been there a number of times. I asked her would it be okay if I checked it out to see if he was there or had been there. She told me the location, the key was at the top of the door but the house could be open because there's no one around that area and it's in the woods. I told her that I'd get back with her as soon as I checked it out and then she said she decided that she didn't want Nathan back just her jewelry. I told her I'd try to locate both and she could handle Nathan anyway she liked.

An hour later I was on my way up Highway 95, two hours and 15 minutes later I found the dirt road Mrs. Studier told me about with just a plain sign with the Studier name and number on it. 30 minutes after that I found the cabin. She was right about one thing, it was in the middle of nowhere. Log cabin about 1200 ft.^{2}. Wraparound screen in porch. The area around the cabin was cleared out and there was a shed to the right of the cabin. There also was a black Packard parked right near the shed with its front driver's window rolled down. I parked and had a good look around before I got out. Got out the car and walked up to the door. I knocked, waited a minute but no one answered so I knocked again.

Waited two, three more minutes and tried the door. It didn't open so I walked around to the back door knocked again. Still no answer, this door was also locked. I then remembered the key over the door reached up over the door frame, no key. I went back to the front door and search there, no key. I walked over to the window looked in and saw what looked like a man's body on the floor, I tried the window and found it was open.

I raise the window climbed up and halfway through, that's when the lights went out. A while later I woke up still lying half in and half out the window. I pulled myself the rest of the way in and set on the floor and felt my head that was throbbing something awful.

When I brought my hand back it had blood on it, damn, what else can go wrong? I got up off the floor and looked around, I noticed a 2-foot statue of a young boy pissing on the floor where my head had been. The place was empty except for the body that was on the floor in the kitchen, I kind of knew who it was before I looked. By the description of him it had to be none other than Nathan Bold. Facedown mouth and eyes wide open with a kitchen knife in his back. I went through his pockets and took out his wallet, all his ID was there including his driver's license. He also had $600 in cash, I took that. What the hell, he didn't need it. Well at least I knew it wasn't robbery, by someone other than me that is.

My guess is Sylvia wasted him and took the jewelry, I took a quick look outside and just as I figured, the

Packard was gone. It was a little past dusk so I knew I had been out at least an hour or more. I took a quick look through of the cabin to maybe find where Sylvia may have run off to, after all she still has to get rid of the jewelry. I did find a bar and help myself to a drink or two. I would have called the police but places out in the boondocks like this one, no one wants to be bothered when they get a place like this anyway, so no phone.

The police would just get shit wrong, maybe even blame me. They all have what seem to be tunnel vision.

 By the time I got back to the city it was near 9 PM and I remember I hadn't eaten since that morning so as I was coming in town, I thought of Mama Sue's. She had a little place that served Home Cooked Meals.

Greens, lima beans, macaroni and cheese, cornbread, yams, pig feet, tails and ears. You know what I'm talking about. Mama Sue's has been at the same location like forever, Euclid, and Cedar. She was a big woman who love to cook and love everybody and everybody loved her. Her moto is; you'll never go away hungry from Mama Sue's!

When I left there all I was looking for was a place to lay my head, I was stuffed.

My head had stopped bleeding and stopped throbbing, almost. I decided to head back to the office to see if any calls came in. In the office I checked by Rita's desk for any messages she would have left me and walked back to my desk, took my bottle out the bottom drawer and poured two fingers.

When the phone rang it kind of startled me, I was deep in thought about the case, where was Sylvia? That is the question. Hello, Ruben here.

Ruben this is Freda, where you ever going to call me?

I was Freda but I have been a little tied up, what's up?

I was wondering if you could come over tonight, I miss you.

Well that's nice that you miss me but you know how I am when I'm on a case, and it's only been what, three days since I last saw you. Plus, I'm really not in the best mood to be with anyone.

Ruben are you okay, you don't sound to swell.

I'm okay Freda this case just getting me down (and the ass kicking from bullet, the knock upside the head at the cabin) didn't help any. But I didn't tell her that.

Tell you what, how about I promise to see you in the next few days.

I'm going to hold you to that Ruben, Freda said.

Freda stayed Way cross town and after that trip to the cabin, hit on the head and dinner at mama sues I'm beat. I don't even think drawls could pick me up.

Rita woke me the next morning and said, you making this a regular thing aren't you, don't you ever go home?

Don't look like it does it Rita. I set up on the couch, stretched and said. But before I could utter a word Rita said, coffee will be ready in five.

After washing up, no change of clothes so that's out. Have to make do with what I have. Rita brought my coffee to the desk and I put a little nip in it, have to start the day off right.

Ten that morning I received a call from Dodie, Ruben I got some news for you man, I heard you been looking for that dude that's married to the Studier woman, how much is it worth to you if I tell you where they are?

We are talking about the Nathan Bold aren't we dodie? Sure, Ruben I know the guy, even seen him with the woman a time or two. Now how much?

I'll tell you what dodie, if you can point him out to me it'll be worth $50.

$50, damn Ruben, you mean that.

Tell me where he is and I'll meet you there. Dodie told me where to meet him in the next hour and I hung up. Now, what kind of game is Dodie trying to play? Unless Nathan is back from the dead that's a safe 50 bucks I won't have to pay. But I'll play!

I reached in the top drawer of my desk and took out my 38 Smith & Wesson, never can be too careful. I had a holster made especially for the piece that fit on my belt in my back. I've seen a couple of guys put theirs in their back without a holster and end up shooting themselves in the ass. Not me, I need my ass. I saw the lights when I made my right-hand turn and I pull the Buick over to the side of the street, put the car in first gear and turned off the engine. I stayed in the car with my hands on the steering wheel. Here we go again I told myself, you would think these police would get tired of these games. Let's see, what's it going to be this time, busted stop light, license plates blocked, or ran a stop sign. They'll come up with something. The two white police officers approach my car on both sides, driver's-side and the passenger side.

The one at the driver's side asked me, driver's license, is this your car?

Yes, it is I said.

You have the papers on this car?

Yes, I do I said.

How could you afford a car like this he said?

Just lucky I guess officer, I said.

What are you doing in this neighborhood? Before Ruben could answer the officer, said, Ruben Kane, that you?

Sure, is officer.

The reason I stopped you Mr. Kane is that you didn't stop at that last stop sign, were you aware of that?

No, I wasn't officer I must have had my mind on that job Mrs. Studier put me on. Mrs. Studier! The Mrs. Studier of Highland Park?

One and the same officer.

The one officer looked across the car to the other and motion him back to their patrol car. What you think Pete? The one said to the other. If this guy is telling the truth and he really is working for Mrs. Studier then we may be setting our self-up for trouble. I don't know about her but the old man can be a bitch. I don't even think we should call the house and check for fear of them thinking we're interfering in their business, the other officer said. Let's just say we never stop this nigger at all, agree? Agreed. The one officer took Rubens driver's license back to his car and hand them to him and said, sorry I stopped you sir, but watch those stop signs.

Ruben said he would and drove off.

It never fails, come up with a big-name white person in town and they back off every time, no balls. If it weren't Studier, I had a few other names I could have called on. Games!

I met Dodie at a vacant warehouse on the river, he's telling me he saw both Nathan and Sylvia go in that building and he saw a light go on the fifth floor. Okay I said let's go! (I didn't question him about being able to see a light that far up in daylight).

I'll wait down here dodie said, you don't need me. Just give me my 50 bucks.

No dodie I said, I think you better come along with me, and I pushed him toward the building entrance. After walking up to the fifth floor we got to the door that dodie saw the light go on. Here it is he said. Now if you don't mind, I'll just get the hell out of here.

You can go dodie, right after you open and go through that door. Look Ruben he said. I pulled out the 38 and said open the got damn door.

Dodie turned the knob and open the door about an inch and I pushed him in the rest of the way. As soon as dodie went through the door something came down hard on his head and he went to the floor. Immediately two burly men were on his ass with what looked like Cleveland Indians baseball bats. After about a minute of them beaten the hell out of dodie I shot one in the leg and the beating stopped. The other guy still had his bat in the air and I told him, I still have another bullet here for you. He dropped his bat and started to stand up but I told him not to do that, just sit there on the floor. And he did.

I think a few questions are in order. I was speaking to the one I hadn't shot the other one was laying on his back holding his leg and moaning.

First, who are you and why you won't to do me?

Nothing personal Mr. It's all business, it's all about the dollar bill.

Name, Ruben said.

Kochi and his name is little bit.

Who sent you Ruben asked?

Bullet! Kochi said. He said that he wanted to put you in the hospital bed next to him. How did dodie get involved?

Bullet said dodie knew everybody and he could probably set you up, just give him a few dollars.

What about Nathan and Sylvia?

Bullet told us you were looking for them and we should try that angle first, other than that, that's all we know Kochi said. One more question Ruben said. How much were you paid?

$200 each Kochi said and he wanted it done as quickly as possible.

Were you aware of the consequences if you fail Ruben said?

We didn't think we would, Kochi said. Kochi today is your lucky day; I'm feeling generous but first give me the money that Bullet paid you two. After receiving the four hundred dollars he shot him in his right knee cap and Kochi screamed.

When he left the warehouse, two men were moaning and in pain laying on the floor and the other was out cold, dead as far as I know.

I stop at a phone booth and call Rita, she told me she got a call from a fellow by the name of Ron Johnson and he heard you were looking for Sylvia. He just saw her going into a pawn shop on the west side of town. He left his phone number. That's great Rita what is it? WH- 7182 got it Rita, thanks. I put another nickel in the slot, dial and listen.

Hello Ron, this is Ruben. What you got on Sylvia?

Yeah Ruben, I saw your girl going into the E&B pawnshop over on the west side, eighth and Savoy, you know where it is?

I do, was she with anyone Ron?

No, she was alone but she was driving a big black Packard. She's probably gone by now.

Probably so but it's still worth a looksee, thanks Ron, what I owe you?

Not a thing Ruben, you helped one of my friends a while back and I'm just returning the favor.

At the pawnshop I talked to the broker and he told me that a girl fitting Silvio's description did come in their trying to sell a few pieces of jewelry, I told her that the stuff she had was to high-class for my shop but I did buy two pieces from her but to tell you the truth I underpaid for them, she said she didn't care, just needed enough money to get home.

Have any idea where she went to from here Ruben said.

None at all the broker said.

Damn, what's next Ruben thought I'm just about out of ideas. Let me call Rita again I think she's still at the office. Rita, this is me, any calls? You just caught me boss, I was just walking out the door. You received a call from T and he wants you to call him, it's about Sylvia.

Did he leave a number Ruben said?

No, he didn't but I would assume he's at the club.

Thanks Rita, I'll try there.

T this is Ruben, you got information about Sylvia?

Yeah Ruben, a couple of my guys just picked her up a little while ago at the bus station parking lot, Nathan wasn't with her, and I'll catch up with him later.

I didn't want to tell him, that won't be happening. Do I get a chance to talk to her? You better get to her quick because I'm going to whip her mother jumping ass and that's no joke. Where are you holding her Ruben asked?

A boarding house on the east side, 536 Roman and Candle Street apartment number six. But Ruben don't arrive before 11 tonight, I need to let my boys go and then have a little talk with her before you get there. She is going to be able to talk isn't she, Ruben said?

I can wait for you Ruben, T said.

A few more hours until I See T and Sylvia so I guess its dinnertime, may not get a chance to eat again tonight. The thing about Cleveland is that they have a bunch of eating places, whatever you like you just have to know where to go get it, and I know. I've been living in Cleveland all my life and tonight I have a taste for some fish, catfish.

Pearls is at the tip of downtown and the beginning of the East side or better known as the Negro section, so they had a clientele of both, East side and Middletown mostly white section, but at pearls that food is what brought us all together. The restaurant had its bar as you walk in but it didn't serve drinks, strictly food. The other side had booths 4 to 6 people could sat and look out the window if that was your thing. Me, I like to eat at the counter, so I can see my food being cooked. Catfish, mac & cheese, coleslaw, roles and coffee. That's what I'm talking bout. Since they didn't serve alcohol at pearls, I had to find a place to get an after-dinner drink, since I still had a couple of hours to kill. I think Worms would be the place to go, small out of the way place. A place you want to go when you rather be alone, to thank. Or have a woman you wanted to keep under cover or you were trying to avoid. Only a select few knew where this place was. When I walked in my table where I always sit was vacant, it was in a corner where you could eye the whole room without them having a good look at you, and on the table was a candle the other tables in the place were set up similar. Lights down low and very intimate. The waitress came over and I ordered my usual, Jim bean on the rocks. I stretch my legs out under the table and picked up my drink and swirl the ice around a few times before I took a drink. I thought about what had happened the last few days and what I was about to run into tonight. Silvia almost made it but now there's no telling what T is going to put on her. I sure hope he lets me talk to her first, I still need to find the jewelry. As I was thinking about all this, I happen to notice the couple across the way at the next table. They were very close whispering in each other's ear, drinking out of each other's glass. From where I set you could definitely see that they were into each other. Oh, to be like that again, love like that only comes around once in a lifetime. I felt envious.

The couple got up to leave, he helped her with her jacket and she kissed him on his cheek. As they were leaving out the lounge, they had to pass under the entrance light, and I could see the couple fairly well. I could see them holding hands and she looking back at him and smiled, and I've seen that look on women's faces before, it says (not too long now). The woman That was whispering in this guy's ear, drinking out of his glass, and kissing him on his cheek.

I knew that woman.

It was then that I realized that the woman I was looking at was my very own wife.

A little after eleven I arrived at apartment # 6 off Savoy Street, a four-story and it was on the second floor, no elevator of course so I walked up. When I reach the door, it was open about an inch, enough for me to pep in anyway and I saw someone laying on the floor. I took out the 38 and walked in, looking around as I did so. The place only had one bedroom, closet, kitchen living room, that together and a bathroom. Living room was a mess, table lamps curtains radio bedroom all turned over. I covered all these before I looked at the body. When I did all I could do was shake my head and said. Damn! Damn! There was T with a kitchen knife in his back, he wasn't looking so good now. I went through his pockets, retrieved his wallet but I didn't find his car keys. He had $1500 in his wallet, I took that, and T would have wanted me to have it. Sylvia's been a very busy young lady (and I did suspect Sylvia). two kills in as many days, WOW! The way I summarize it, T got to the apartment and started beating on that ass and somehow Sylvia got the upper hand and put it to him when his back was turned. Score another one for Sylvia. I think she took T's car but she should know she won't get very far in that because everyone knows it and will be on the lookout for a 1938 Buick with T-man on the back bumper, Just as soon as they find the body. But again, I found no jewelry, then I got to thinking when T's men picked her up was it before or after she left the bus parking lot. If they picked her up while she was still in the car then maybe the jewelry's still with the Packard and if that's so she'll most likely head back to the bus station parking lot.

Sounds like a plan to me, I'm thinking the killing didn't happen too long ago so I've got a good chance of catching her there. Two blocks from the bus station I spotted T's car parked but no Sylvia so I figured she ditched the car and is walking the rest of the way to the station. When I pull up on her she was just closing the door of the Packard and getting ready to leave. I pulled in behind her so she would be blocked in and got out of my car with the 38 in hand. With her having two kills the last couple of days I wasn't taking any chances. She hadn't had time to start the car but her windows were rolled up and doors locked. I mention for her to roll down the window and reluctantly she did.

Sylvia, I said. Give me the jewelry!

I, Sylvia said.

I really don't want to hear no shit I said. You see, I know about Nathan at the cabin and I also know about T, so Sylvia please don't give me no shit.

What do I get in return if I give them to you?

I cocked the 38 and looked at her. She reached under the passenger side of the front seat and brought out a jewelers case and hand it to me. I would have said thank you but what the hell man, she had just killed two men. I took the case and started walking toward my car,

Sylvia said hey, is that it, you're not turning me in to the police or anything? That's not what I was hired for but you did kill a friend of mine, of course it may have been self-defense but Nathan's wasn't.

Some advice to you Sylvia, Run, run fast and run far. My guess is Bullet will be coming after you and soon.

The butler opened the door and I said. Ruben Kane for Mrs. Studier.

Yes, she is expecting you Mr. Kane. Come in, can I take your hat?

No thanks, I won't be here that long.

Mrs. Studier is in the study, up the hall way, first room on the left.

The study would make four of my two room office, high dollar pictures on the wall, couches and chairs were worth a small fortune. Fireplace, flowers, (the real ones) and a bar almost the size of the one at the ebony club, on a smaller scale that is.

Mr. Kane, good to see you, you have good news for me?

Well Mrs. Studier I have good news and bad. First the good news and I handed her the jewelry case. Everything is there I believe except a couple of pieces and there at the pawnshop, I could pick them up for you if you like.

And the bad news Mr. Kane?

Nathan is dead, I said. And I went on to tell her the who, where and when. She took it well, had me to pick up the pieces at the pawn shop, and paid me a substantial amount far above my fee. Thanked me and my job was done.

Sunday morning a week later at breakfast drinking coffee Ruben was reading the sports section, his wife was sitting across from him reading the obituary and said. Did you read where Tonelli got killed? You remember him don't you? Didn't you two go to the same school?

Yeah, I said and continued reading the sports.

I also see where that Nathan boy was found dead, wasn't he that Negro who married the rich white woman?

I guess Ruben said and continued reading. Damn he said, the Indians lost again!

Ruben finish with the sports section and picked up the front page, Tonelli and Nathan was on the third page they were only given eight lines each. Negros found dead with knife in the back, no suspects. Negroes never do get much of a headline. Then Ruben spotted something that made him perk up, an article on the last page. Outside Chicago a Negro was found hanging from a telephone pole after he was caught cutting the throat of a white woman. The Negro had driver's license with a Cleveland Ohio address, his name was Robert Marshall (39).

Bullet! I said to myself.

End